A FRIEND INDEED

TRUE TALES OF DOG HEROISM
D.J. ARNESON

A GROLIER COMPANY

Franklin Watts
New York/London/Toronto/Sydney/1981

These real-life stories have been adapted from ac-
tual accounts of the annual Ken-L Ration Dog Hero
Awards program winners furnished by the Ken-L
Ration Division of Quaker Oats, Inc. whose assist-
ance is gratefully acknowledged.

Photographs by permission of
The Quaker Oats Company

Library of Congress Cataloging in Publication Data

Arneson, D J
A friend indeed.

SUMMARY: Eight true stories of
unusual heroism exhibited by dogs who have won
the Gold Medal for Dog Hero of the Year.
1. Dogs—Legends and stories. [1. Dogs]
I. Title. II. Title: Dog heroism.
SF426.5.A73   818'.5403   80–23062
ISBN 0–531–04257–X

CONTENTS

A GOLD MEDAL FOR TANG
3

LADY
19

PATCHES
31

HERO
41

MIJO
53

RINGO
61

A DOG NAMED GRIZZLY
73

TRIXIE
85

A GOLD MEDAL
FOR TANG
1954

The four neighborhood children paused beneath the shade of a large tree. The sun was hot and bright in the clear blue sky over Denison, Texas, yet the grass surrounding the tree was cool and pleasant. It felt good on bare feet.

The tree was on a small hill overlooking a peaceful glen. It was a popular spot for kids to gather, especially on a summer Saturday.

Three of the friends—Kim, Mary, and Pete— had visited the shady glen many times. Only Todd, new to Denison, had never been there before. While his friends stretched out on the inviting grass to cool off, Todd stood by the thick trunk of the tree and looked around. A shiny white stone in the quietest part of the glen caught his eye. It sparkled in the sunlight, as white as a patch of snow on the green, green grass.

"What's that down there?" Todd asked his friends.

Kim raised herself up on one elbow. She squinted as a stray slip of sunshine winked at her through the dark leaves above her head. A look of sadness crossed her face when she saw the white stone. She knew very well what it was. She sat up.

"It's a gravestone," Kim said quietly.

Mary and Pete, on hearing Kim's words, stopped talking and also sat up. Their eyes went straight to the small stone thirty feet away.

Todd took a short step in that direction.

"A *gravestone?*" he asked, not quite sure he had heard right.

The three others stood and joined him.

"Mmm hmm," Pete answered.

"But what's it doing *here?*" Todd asked, more puzzled than ever now that he knew he had heard right. "I mean, who would they bury out here?" He turned toward the small neighborhood, where his own house and the houses of his friends could be seen only a short distance away, baking in the summer sun.

Mary touched Todd's arm. "Come on," she said in a low voice, "we'll show you."

The four descended the hill. The first, somber feelings that Mary, Pete, and Kim had felt when reminded of the presence of the gravestone were replaced by a growing sense of pride. They quickened their pace until they were almost at a run.

Pete, always the fastest of the group, reached the stone first. He waited for the others. Todd, a little reluctant to invade such a private place, was the last to arrive. He looked down at the stone. It was not very large, not much larger, in fact, than the dictionary on the teacher's desk at school. It was also not very ornately decorated. On its front were carved just three words, that was all. Todd read them aloud.

"Tang. A Hero."

The three longtime friends nodded silently. Todd waited. "Well, who is Tang?" he finally asked. His interest was growing by the moment.

Mary kneeled on the grass next to the small grave marker. She brushed a bit of dust from its top. But it was as though she were petting it rather than dusting it. Her hand moved lovingly over the cool marble. Kim settled next to her, and Pete sat down, too.

"Tang was a dog," Mary said simply, looking up at Todd. "Sit down and we'll tell you all about him."

Todd sat down and crossed his legs in Indian fashion. The four friends formed a small circle around the smooth, snow-white stone.

Mary, who was the oldest of the group and had lived in the neighborhood the longest, then told Todd the story of Tang.

Tang was a big, fluffy, unusually friendly brown-and-white collie. He was the special pet of Captain Dyer and his wife, who lived in a house just down the street from where the four friends were sitting. Captain Dyer was in the air force.

The Dyers had lived in Denison for several years, ever since Captain Dyer's transfer to Perrin Air Force Base only a few miles away. Before they moved to Denison, the Dyers were stationed in Alaska. That's where Tang was born.

Tang wasn't the Dyers' first dog. In fact, he wasn't even their first collie. They had had another dog, a dearly loved pet who had died. As much as they loved dogs, neither Captain nor Mrs. Dyer could bear the thought of adopting another to replace their cherished pet. They both agreed that a new dog would remind them too much of their favorite.

Then a friend of theirs, a veterinarian, mentioned that he knew of a collie puppy that was available for adoption. The Dyers at first refused to even consider it. But the vet, a good judge of people as well as of dogs, persisted. He knew the Dyers would be the perfect couple to adopt the tiny pup. He talked them into taking "just one little look" at the furry brown-and-white collie.

The Dyers agreed to just one look, nothing more.

The collie was not quite what they expected. Even though he was still only a puppy, the dog the vet showed the Dyers was completely mistrustful of humans. Children, in particular, caused the dog to turn unfriendly and go on his guard to protect himself. It was evident that already in his young life, the pup had been seriously mistreated. To adopt such a dog would surely be a mistake. The air base housing where the Dyers lived was like a small town. It had streets, houses, and lots of people coming and going. But more than that, the streets and sidewalks were crowded with children. A dog who mistrusted adults *and* youngsters in a place like that would be miserable, to say nothing of its owners.

But something happened on that day when the Dyers took "just one look" at the poor maltreated pup. Smaller than a furry mop on the end of a stick, the pup looked back. And something in his eyes captured the Dyers from that moment on. That special something, so very much like the dog they had lost, reached out and touched the Captain and his wife.

And so, with a smile and a lot of misgivings, they took the frightened puppy in their arms and carried him home.

The Dyers named their new puppy Tang. They showered him with love and affection. He became very special to them. The fear and mistrust that Tang showed in the beginning began to melt away. As he grew by leaps and bounds, getting bigger and stronger each day, his behavior toward people changed. Within six months there wasn't a trace of mistrust left in him. He was a big, powerful dog, and a very friendly one as well. In fact, he became so friendly that even though he was completely untrained, he assumed the role of guardian for the children living on the base.

The air force base was a busy place. Naturally,

the skies were never empty. But neither were the streets. Trucks, cars, and buses were constantly on the go, moving men and women, equipment, and supplies from place to place. Often the streets in front of the homes where the base personnel lived were dangerously busy. Tang, full-grown by now, watched the traffic with a canny eye whenever there were children playing near the street.

One day in spring when it was warm enough to play outdoors, Mrs. Dyer happened to be watching Tang from the window of her house while Tang himself was watching a group of neighborhood children near the street. Three of the youngsters were drifting toward the road. They were more interested in their play than in watching where they were going. Mrs. Dyer felt uncomfortable seeing the children so close to the road. She decided to call out to them to warn them away from the curb.

Just then a large truck loaded with oil drums entered the street. Mrs. Dyer hurried toward the door of her house, intending to rush outside and call the children to safety.

But Tang also heard the truck. He dashed to the street and quickly placed himself between the children and the roadway. None of the three realized what the keen-eyed dog was doing. They simply moved back up onto the sidewalk because it was easier than trying to get around the bushy-tailed collie who scooted back and forth, blocking their way into the street. The truck rumbled noisily by without incident.

Mrs. Dyer saw it all. She sighed with relief and praised the day she and her husband had decided to adopt Tang.

Perhaps the lesson that day wasn't strong enough to impress the small group of neighborhood youngsters whom Tang had chosen to protect, because the same thing happened again and again. Whenever a child or group of children worked their way too near the road, Tang would shepherd them back to safety. Many never even realized they had been in danger.

Then one murky day, when the sky was gray and the air had turned chill, Tang performed his first act of true heroism.

A small boy, younger than the rest of the neighborhood gang, had wandered away from the group. None of the children noticed the boy was missing because they were too busy playing "Red Light, Green Light" on the Dyers' front lawn.

Again Mrs. Dyer happened to be watching out the window when a car entered the street much faster than it should have. It was halfway down the block before she saw the stray child wandering directly into the car's path. The driver, it was clear, did not see the child.

Tang's fur bristled at the sound of the speeding car. He turned toward the street. His clear eyes spotted the car and the child. In seconds the unsuspecting youngster would be hit.

Mrs. Dyer screamed. But she was still inside the house, and her warning was unheard.

But no shout of warning was necessary for Tang. With fur flying, the brave dog bounded into the street. He raced straight into the path of the oncoming car.

Wasting no time or energy barking, he dashed to the child and pushed him with all of his might. At the powerful thrust of the big dog, the child stumbled aside.

The car whizzed past—so close that Tang's long, graceful tail whipped violently in the wind. But the child was safe.

Mrs. Dyer closed her eyes in relief. Never in her life was she more grateful that she had taken that "one little look" at the frightened, abused puppy she now lovingly called Tang.

Yet Tang's heroics didn't end with that life-saving incident. Soon after, a similar situation developed on the same street. Another child had wandered into the street, and again, nobody noticed before it was too late. For the second time in his life, Tang ran into the street and risked his own life in front of a speeding car to shove the child to safety.

Tang became famous among the children and parents at the Alaskan air force base. Parents felt more secure when Tang was romping with their children. And why shouldn't they? He had already saved two from serious injury and possible death.

And then, sadly for all of those in the neighborhood who knew him, children and adults alike, Tang's master and mistress were transferred by the air force to Texas. Friends and neighbors wished the Dyers and their remarkable dog a safe trip. They were all thankful for his brave deeds.

But a guardian dog is a guardian dog for life. Collies, bred for centuries into perfect shepherds, have an instinct to protect their flock. For Tang, his flock was children. And so, when the Dyers moved to Denison, Texas, another neighborhood of youngsters benefited by the sleekly groomed collie's presence.

It was in Denison that Mary met Tang. She lived in the neighborhood, not too far from the Dyers' house. Peter and Kim also became friends of Tang's because the faithful guardian immediately took up his old habits and began playing nursemaid and baby-sitter to all the children in the neighborhood.

Tang's fame began to spread through the small town. He became a fixture among groups of children who, like those in Alaska and perhaps everywhere, sometimes played too near the street.

Mrs. Dyer saw it coming. It was like the replay of a bad dream. A little girl was wandering next to the road. She held a red rubber ball in her hand. Somehow the ball scooted from her grip. It rolled off the curb and into the street. The child followed it, laughing at the way it bounced from the curb into the street, as if it were trying to escape from her.

Tang's fur bristled the way it always did when he sensed danger. It didn't make any difference if a car was coming or not. To him, seeing a child straying into the street aroused his instincts to a fever pitch. His ancestors before him would not allow a lamb to wander from their flock, and Tang would not allow a child to wander from his.

But a car *was* coming! Tang raced at top speed toward the road. His paws barely touched the ground. His long fur flew straight back.

By the time the driver saw the child, it was too late to turn the car. A fearful screech of brakes split the air in the normally quiet neighborhood. Mothers froze in horror at the sound. And Mrs. Dyer, dashing from her house to scream a warning, froze at the terrifying sight.

But Tang leaped into the air. His broad chest smacked soundly into the child as she bent down to pick up the mischievous ball. The little girl tumbled backwards under the impact and rolled safely into the gutter, much too frightened and surprised to cry.

When the startled child sat up, she was surrounded by people. Every home within earshot of the screeching brakes had emptied. The sight of all the people scared the child. She began to cry. But she was safe.

Mrs. Dyer knelt next to Tang, who stood at the little girl's side until she was swept up into her mother's arms. "You are more than a friend," the mother said to the stalwart dog. "You're a *hero!*"

There wasn't a soul in Denison who would disagree. News of Tang's heroism spread quickly throughout the town.

But even then the fearless Tang didn't let up.

It was a sleepy Texas morning. The heat had not yet risen. Denison was still basking under pleasant blue skies. There were a few puffy clouds scattered from one end of the flat horizon to the other. Tang was lying in the shade on the cool front step of the Dyers' house.

A familiar sound in the neighborhood broke the quiet. The white-and-red milk delivery truck of the local dairy entered the street. It stopped at the house on the corner lot at the end of the block. The milkman disappeared into the back of the truck for a moment. When he reappeared, his hand held a basket filled with containers of milk and cream and a carton of fresh eggs. He hurried up the walk to the house, left his customer's order, and returned to the truck. He then drove two houses further up the block and repeated his movements.

But while the milkman was at the rear entrance to his next customer's house, out of sight of the street and his parked truck, a little girl in a bright yellow T-shirt, blue jeans, and sneakers entered the street. She had been playing in her yard. The gaily colored truck attracted her attention. Tang saw her at once. Ever watchful, there was scarcely a moment when the movement of a child on his street didn't catch his eye. His ears perked up. His eyes followed the child as she wandered across the empty street toward the truck and disappeared behind it.

When the little girl didn't reappear, Tang got

to his feet. He trotted toward the truck at the same time that the milkman was returning from behind the house. The milkman knew Tang. He smiled at him as they passed.

Tang hurried to the curb. He stepped quickly into the street and went to the rear of the truck. The little girl was still there. She was perched precariously high on the rear bumper of the truck. The bumper was nothing more than a narrow steel ledge. Once the truck started forward, the child would tumble headfirst onto the hard, paved street.

The truck's engine roared as the driver prepared to move to his next customer. Tang let out a sharp bark and raced to the front of the truck. He stopped directly in the path of the big truck and began barking madly.

The driver shouted at Tang to get out of the way. He had a schedule to keep. Besides that, he had enough trouble trying to keep from waking the whole neighborhood with his truck. A loudly barking dog didn't help matters at all.

Tang refused to budge. He yelped and barked. The driver gunned the engine to scare the big brown-and-white dog aside, but Tang held firm. The driver was plainly annoyed. However, seeing that the collie was determined to outlast him in this contest of wits, he turned off the engine and stepped into the street. He muttered at Tang, who continued to bark. Apparently, it wasn't enough to merely get out of the truck.

The driver put his hands on his hips and stared

angrily at the strange-acting dog. Tang barked as loud as ever. The driver's anger slowly began to give way to wonder. After all, he knew Tang and he knew Tang's reputation. Though he wasn't quite sure why, he turned away from the barking dog and walked to the rear of his truck. Cold sweat broke out on his brow when he saw the little girl balanced on the high bumper. He reached for her and, grasping her tightly in his strong hands, placed her safely on the sidewalk, well away from the street and the shiny truck.

The moment the little girl's feet touched the sidewalk, Tang stopped barking and trotted nonchalantly back to his place in the cool shade at the front of his owners' house.

Yet even that heroic deed wasn't the last of Tang's remarkable exploits.

On another day, for the fourth time in his life, Tang bolted into the street in front of a speeding car just in the nick of time to push two more children to safety. Four times! Five lives! Four times the dog who had been abused as a puppy by children and adults had risked his own life to rescue children who might otherwise have been injured or killed. The little girl on the back of the milk truck was the sixth child he had saved from real danger; there were many more he had shepherded to safety away from the street, before danger could come.

The people of Denison were proud of Tang. He was a real celebrity. But the biggest day of his life was still to come.

A national award for dog heroes had just been established. Its purpose was to recognize the daring feats of dogs like Tang who risked danger to save lives. Each year there are numerous acts of bravery by dogs, and it was agreed that the time had come to acknowledge them. Tang's name and exploits were submitted to the judges, who would determine from among all of the entrants which dog would be named Dog Hero of the Year.

Tang won! His remarkable acts of lifesaving were instantly recognized as outstanding. And in a ceremony fit for a real hero, just what he was, Tang was presented with the first-ever Gold Medal for dog heroism!

"And when he came home," Mary said, with a memory of that long-ago day still fresh in her mind, "all of us kids in the neighborhood got together and gave him a parade."

"It was just like the kind they give to heroes," Peter added proudly, "because Tang was the greatest hero of them all."

After a few moments of silence, the four friends arose and disappeared over the hill. The wind blew softly through the tree on the hilltop and swept down toward the grave marker, stirring the grass as it passed. The white stone was once again alone. But it was not forgotten.

LADY
1959

The blue-and-white van of the St. Louis Telephone Company slowed as it climbed a lonely hilltop on the border of Mehlville, Missouri, and then pulled to a stop on the shoulder of the abandoned road. Two men, linemen for the company, were inside.

"Do you want to check that street guide again, Bill?" Chuck Moore asked his partner from behind the wheel of the van. He peered down the empty street. A line of tall poles stood like sentries on one side of the vacant thoroughfare, supporting a sparse collection of wires at their tops. The telephone lines curved in gentle drooping arcs from one pole to the next. "There's no sign of a break as far as I can see," he said, squinting to focus his sight on the farthest of the poles.

Bill Yerke unfolded a large street guide and map on his knees. His fingers ran over the area they had just traveled. "We've covered every street on the grid," he said, glancing out the window to confirm that the van was where he had marked with his finger. He shook his head. "If there's a line down here somewhere, there's only one other place to look." He turned to face directly out the side window. "Out there," he said with a grimace.

Chuck Moore shrugged his shoulders and turned off the ignition. The van's engine sputtered to a stop. A deathly silence filled the air. The remoteness of the countryside cast a thick blanket of quiet over the men and the van as perceptible as the low-scudding, black-and-gray February clouds that filled the winter sky. The clouds blew east, over the van and toward the uninviting hills and marshes that lay off to the side of the road. A single spur of telephone wire, held high off the ground by a row of weathered poles, could be seen trailing off into the distance through the rolling, uninhabited land. "Nice day for a hike," Chuck said as he opened his door and stepped onto the road, his shoulders hunching against the chill air. "Better take a jacket." He then headed for the rear of the van, to get the equipment he and Bill would need to repair the downed line, once it was found.

The two men worked in practiced unison. Partners and friends, they were familiar with the routine. Soon they were on their way over the first hill, following the poles one by one. Their yellow vinyl foul-weather boots flopped noisily over the dry grass. These would come in handy once they reached the low-lying swamps and murky marshes they knew awaited them further inside this undeveloped stretch of Missouri countryside.

"C'mon Lady. We take a walk." Three-year-old Tommy Abel waited at the edge of the yard for his dog. "C'mon," he said impatiently, "just me 'n you."

Lady trotted to Tommy's side. A mixed breed of half collie and half shepherd, Lady's thick tan-and-white coat ruffled in the bitter wind that blew through the yard. The pure white "boots" of her forepaws padded quietly over the ground. She was well protected against the midwinter chill. Tommy stroked his mittened hand over Lady's glossy coat. "Let's go," he said.

The little boy and dog soon reached the sidewalk that ran along the front yards of the suburban homes of the neighborhood. The dog stood nearly as high as her young master. Tommy paused for a moment and then headed north, toward the empty spaces that lay behind the last of the houses. It was a cold, unfriendly, stay-at-home February day, and nobody saw the pair trudge quietly up the block and leave the familiar surroundings of the neighborhood for the low rolling hills and backcountry beyond.

Tommy ran over the top of a hill and into the knee-high, bone-dry grass. The grass made a rustling sound as it brushed against his legs. He laughed. At his side, Lady trotted easily on four flying feet, her mouth open to taste the air, her eyes glancing from side to side. But never once did she let her young master disappear from view. For even though Lady was a mongrel, her instincts were all shepherd.

Looking down from high overhead, a single jet-black crow fought its way against the wind. From the air the countryside below was an unbroken expanse of knoblike hills and wet, low-lying marshes. The city of St. Louis was far, far off. Even the houses and streets of Mehlville were no longer close by. The little boy and his dog, looking no larger than ants against the yellow-gray grass, were blocks and blocks from civilization—and safety. The crow flew off, but Tommy and Lady trotted on.

Tommy suddenly stopped. The bright, curious smile on his face that had marked the start of his and Lady's adventure faded. He glanced from side to side. Then he twisted his head to look all around. He and Lady were at the edge of a swampy, flat, open area surrounded by low hills. Each direction looked the same. There was no sun in the sky, only dark clouds that grew darker as the sun, somewhere behind them, sank lower and lower. It had grown late. And Tommy was hopelessly lost.

"I wanna go home," Tommy moaned, afraid now of the sound of his own voice in the desolate place. He took an unsure step forward, then quickly retreated. The ground was soupy. Thick clay clung to the bottom of his boots. No matter where he put his feet, they sank into the mucky ground. Soon the tops of both of his boots were buried in the stuff. He struggled to free himself, but the movement only drove his feet deeper into the clinging clay. He was soon up to his ankles in it, trapped.

"I wanna go home," he whined again, this time through thick, salty tears that streamed down his ruddy, windblown cheeks. "I wanna go home *now!*" But that wasn't possible. Tommy Abel was firmly held by the earth, out of sight and sound of anyone, in a place no one would even suspect a small boy would be. And if he were not found soon, he would die of exposure during the bitter-cold and fast-approaching night.

"Where's Tommy?"

"Oh, Walter!" Tommy's mother sounded frantic as she met her alarmed husband at the door of their house. "He's gone. I've looked everywhere. He was in the yard with Lady and the next thing I knew, he was gone."

The Abels quickly organized a search party. Shouting the boy's name against the wind and coming darkness, friends, neighbors, and police combed the neighborhood, investigating every nook and cranny and out-of-the-way place a three-year-old boy might hide. Singly and in groups, they hurried up and down the streets of the neighborhood, hoping to find a clue. But every turn led to a dead end, every shout faded, unanswered, to silence, and every lead withered and died. All the while, time and darkness and bitter cold were working against them. And, unknown to any of the searchers, their hunt was taking them further from, rather than closer to, their small, lost quarry.

Lady stood at the edge of the mucky swamp. Her ears twitched attentively each time Tommy whimpered. Her eyes were pinned on her little master as he tried to move. But Tommy was becoming too weak to shout or even to stand. He slumped to the wet ground. "I wanna go home," he sobbed. "I'm cold."

"Rrrff!"

With a sharp bark at the wind, Lady suddenly spun around and streaked to the top of the closest hill. She stopped for a moment to look down into the gloom where Tommy lay in the mud, sobbing and whimpering and unable to move. Then, pointing her long collie nose into the wind, she scampered off the hilltop and was gone.

"What in the devil is all that racket, Bill?" Chuck Moore stood up straight, above the opened equipment bag at his feet. He cocked his ear toward the thick woods that lay off to one side of where he and Bill Yerke were working. "Can you hear it?" he asked.

Bill dug his spikes deep into the soft gray wood of the pole he was climbing and leaned back against the safety of the thick strap secured to his waist and the pole. He listened intently. "Sounds like a dog," he said. Then a moment later, "Sounds hurt."

Chuck shook his head as he closed the top of the equipment bag. "Must have run into a skunk or something, the way he's carrying on. . . . Will you look at *that*—"

The startled lineman was interrupted in midsentence by Lady, who exploded from the woods, wailing at the top of her lungs.

"Mad dog!" Yerke shouted from the safety of his midair perch. Moore leaped for cover. But Lady ran around and around him, barking every step of the way.

"Get him off me," Chuck Moore screamed, even though the dog was posing no threat at all. "Get him away from me, Bill."

Bill Yerke studied Lady for a moment from above. Then he quickly lowered himself to the ground. "He's a she," he said, beckoning to Lady, "and she doesn't appear to be hurt at all. C'mere gal," he called softly.

Lady barked louder than ever. She ran in ever-widening circles, then closed in again and repeated the sequence, scampering farther and farther from the puzzled men and then dashing back to where they stood.

"I don't know about you, Chuck, but I've seen

enough Lassie shows on TV to wonder if maybe she wants us to follow her." Yerke looked at the sky and then at his watch. "What do you think?"

"She sure is acting strange if you ask me," Chuck Moore said. He picked up the equipment bag. "Sure, why not? I can't imagine anybody being out there, though," he said, glancing thoughtfully at the desolate hills and gloomy woods, "but just in case, maybe we better."

The men gathered their equipment and set off behind Lady, who hadn't stopped barking since she found them. They picked up their pace, desperately trying to keep up with the fleet-footed dog. Each time they fell behind, Lady whirled around and circled back to get them.

After twenty minutes of following Lady over hills and through dense woods, Moore stopped. As cold as it was, he wiped a band of sweat from his forehead with his sleeve. "I think she's taking us on a wild goose chase, Bill," he said, puffing from the exertion.

The two men stood at the bottom of a low hill. They had trekked over a half-dozen just like it already and had found nothing. Lady raced around them, filling the air with her sharp barks. She dashed to the top of the hill, paused, looked over to the other side, and then bounded back down to the men.

"OK, girl," Chuck Moore said, picking up his equipment bag again, "just one more hill. That's all. If this is some kind of game you're playing, it's all over as soon as we top this hill. You got it?"

Lady streaked over the crest of the hill. Moore and Yerke puffed up the incline behind her.

"Oh my God!"

Tommy Abel looked up through large, glistening tears at the two men who appeared suddenly at the top of the hill. A wan smile crossed his dirt-streaked face. The men dropped their heavy canvas bags and bounded down the hill toward him. They slogged their way through the yellow clay, quickly freed his feet, and scooped him up, shivering, into their arms. "I wanna go home," he said in a voice no louder than a whisper of wind, " 'n Lady too."

Lady followed the men carrying the cold, frightened boy to their truck. Later, when Tommy was safely home and tucked in bed, snug under his own warm blankets, Lady curled up in a furry heap in a corner of the room, and she too dropped off to sleep, exhausted from her ordeal. But her deed was not forgottten. For saving her young master and for exhibiting unflagging determination and quick, resourceful intelligence, she would be awarded the coveted Gold Medal.

PATCHES
1965

An unusually bitter-cold wind blew over the frigid waters of Lake Spanaway on a dark December night a few days before Christmas. The black water rose and fell in choppy silence as the wind cut through it like an invisible blade. A few flickering lights from lakefront homes, broken up into many tiny points along the shore, could be seen on the dense velvety surface of the water. The raw beauty of the scene, however, was lost upon the homeowners who shared Lake Spanaway. They were snug at home, warmed by fires and furnace, oblivious to the teeth-chattering cold.

Marvin Scott parked his car in the driveway to his home and braced himself for the short, frigid walk to the warmth and comfort of his house. He had worked late that night at his furniture store in town. Now it was nearly ten o'clock. He was eager to get inside to relax with a hot meal and perhaps catch the late news on television. He was very tired.

31

He climbed quickly out of the car and, pulling his coat tightly around him, hurried toward the door.

He stopped midway up the walk. An unpleasant sound—the hollow thump of something banging down by his small dock—came up from the lake. The thumping continued. Mr. Scott frowned. He opened the door to the house and quickly stepped inside.

"My, don't you look cold!" Mrs. Scott said, greeting her husband at the door. "It's no surprise, though," she quickly added. "The weatherman just said it's going to drop to zero later tonight." She shivered at the thought of the cold lurking outside her door.

Marvin Scott took off his glasses. They had fogged up so badly he couldn't see a thing. He wiped them carefully with his handkerchief and stood in the doorway, listening to the now-muffled thumping sound coming from the lake.

"Is something the matter?" Mrs. Scott asked. The look on her husband's face was clearly troubled.

Mr. Scott sighed heavily. He was exhausted from his long day at the store and wasn't at all eager to face the problem on his mind. "I'm afraid we've got ice on the lake," he said, tipping his head to catch the faint sound carried on the wind. "With this wind, if it gets too thick it'll punch a hole right through the patrol boat."

"Can't it wait until morning?" Mrs. Scott asked.

"I don't think so. I'd better take a look now, before I get too comfortable," he answered. He replaced his glasses and returned to the closet, taking down his thickest overcoat.

At that instant there was a flurry of sound, the tap-tapping of hard claws across a hard floor. Mr. Scott grinned broadly as Patches, his black-and-white dog, part collie and part Alaskan malamute, trotted into the hallway. Patches' bushy tail wagged expectantly as his eyes caught his master's eyes. Mr. Scott buttoned his coat under his chin. "Of course you can come," he said in answer to Patches' silent question and leaned down to tousle the big dog's fur with a firm, friendly shake. Patches ran to the door and waited.

"Hurry back, dear," Mrs. Scott said as her hand pulled the neck of her sweater closed, to ward off the chill that would blow into the house from the inky-black night.

"Don't worry," Mr. Scott answered. He opened the door and again clearly heard the sound of the ice bumping against the moored boat. It wasn't going to be a pleasant task. The wind whipped his coat as he headed toward the lake and forced tears from his eyes as it blew bitterly across his face.

Patches, a distant relative of the thick-furred Alaskan malamutes, whose ancestors had lived in the freezing far north with the Malamute Eskimos, had less trouble facing the wind. His fur rippled over like dark waves on a silent lake. He trotted to the lakefront at his master's side, his back straight and his feet firm on the frozen ground. Genetic memories, bred into him from centuries of wolflike forebears, shrugged off the winter chill. He was in his element.

The two soon reached the shoreline. Mr. Scott stepped onto the rough-planked wooden dock jutting into the lake from his property and shook his head. "I was afraid of this," he said to Patches, who stood at his side. "Ice." A thin sheet of ice had formed near the shore. It had already built up around the boat. Left unattended, the ice would form a solid mass and crush the boat in its grip. "I'd better do something or it'll be ruined," he said, looking around in the darkness for something to break the boat free from the ice. He picked up a timber lying at the edge of the dock and pushed at the boat. It wouldn't budge. "It's thicker than I thought," he said aloud, moving closer to the edge of the dock for another try.

What Marvin Scott didn't see was the thin film of ice that had formed on the surface of the dock from water blown there by the wind. His feet rested precariously on the edge of the slippery surface. He gripped the timber tightly in his hands and pushed at the boat with all his might. Suddenly his feet flew out from under him, as if they'd been kicked. He dropped the timber and reached for the sky as he was catapulted off the dock into the frigid black water. As he fell, his legs smashed against the edge of the dock, ripping and tearing muscle and tendon into agonizing uselessness. He screamed in pain as he plunged into the icy, fifteen-foot-deep water. Weighted down by his heavy, water-soaked coat, he went under the moment he hit.

At first, there seemed no hope for survival. Then, with a sharp jerk of his head and pain as if he were being scalped, the doomed man stopped sinking and began to rise. Apparently Patches had leaped into the water the instant Mr. Scott slipped and dived deep to reach the helpless, drowning man. With his jaws clamped together over a thick lock of his master's hair, Patches was now struggling to reach the surface.

For what must have seemed like hours but was only seconds, the valiant dog paddled determinedly upwards, until first he and then the drowning man broke the surface. They were far out in the lake, more than twenty feet from the dock. Mr. Scott—in deep pain, badly dazed by the sudden accident, and numbed by the chilling water—flopped ineffectively on the waves. But the brave dog refused to give up. Still holding to his master with a death grip, Patches paddled desperately for the safety of the shore. Water ran into his mouth, threatening to choke him, and waves splashed over his nose. But still the dog held on. He pitted his own meager eighty-five pounds of rapidly failing strength against the dead weight of a full-grown man and crawled inch by inch through the water until, close to drowning himself, the two were within reach of the ice-covered dock.

Mr. Scott raised his arm limply, reaching through the darkness for the dock. His hand touched the coarse wood and his fingers closed over it. When at last he had a firm hold of the dock, he pulled himself slowly closer to it. Patches then let go of his master and climbed onto the dock, exhausted from his heroic effort.

Scott's legs were useless. The torn tissue had left them bleeding and numb. Scott managed to pull himself halfway onto the dock, but his legs remained hanging limply in the water. The bitter cold sapped what was left of his failing strength. He began to lose his grip. Like a huge fish, the dazed and shaken man slid silently back into the water and again vanished beneath the choppy surface.

For a second time Patches leaped into the water. The brave dog swam to the rapidly sinking man and again clamped his jaws shut over a trailing lock of hair. For a second time the dog struggled upward to the surface with his master. And for a second time the two bobbed up into the bitter winter air, out of reach of the dock. But this time they were only a few feet out. Patches paddled against the wind and waves until Scott could again get a firm grip on the dock. Only when the injured man appeared to be safe from falling back did the valiant dog let go. Then Patches himself began to sink. Exhausted beyond the point of saving himself, the dog drifted helplessly on the water.

Marvin Scott, nearly shocked to numbness by

the sequence of events, was aware that Patches was now in desperate need of help. He pushed the soaked and shivering animal with what remained of his own strength until the dog was finally able to scramble safely out of the water and onto the dock. But now Scott had no strength left to pull himself out. He lay with his legs floating uselessly in the water and only his chest and arms on the dock.

"Help!" the exhausted man yelled weakly, over and over again. But his cries were lost amid the rush of the wind and the chopping of the waves. His strength was nearly gone. To remain any longer in the numbing water would drain him completely. He would soon slip back beneath the waves and this time drown for sure.

Patches whimpered at his master's plight. He struggled to his feet, braced his paws on the icy dock, and reached forward to grasp the thick collar of Scott's overcoat with his teeth. Pulling with the strength that was the pride of his sled-dog heritage, Patches tugged at the injured man's coat.

New hope fueled Scott's will to survive. Gasping for air but determined not to go down for the third time, he at last pulled himself onto the dock with Patches' help. The brave dog didn't let go of the coat collar even when the danger of the man falling back into the water was past. Instead he held his grip and continued to pull as the shivering man crawled inch by inch up the long, rock-studded slope leading to his house. When neither man nor beast could crawl any further, they collapsed, the back door of the house just out of reach.

Scott mustered the last of his fading strength. "Help," he shouted weakly. But again it was useless. His voice by now was reduced to a murmur. Patches lay at his side, too drained of energy and too cold to even bark.

Scott's frozen hands closed over something lying on the ground. Though there was no feeling left in his fingers, he knew it was a stone. He raised his arm weakly, knowing there would be only one chance, and flung the stone forward. It clattered loudly against the kitchen door. In moments a shadow appeared behind the frosty glass. Mrs. Scott, her eyes wide in surprise, rushed to the fallen pair. They were saved.

Marvin Scott hovered between life and death for twenty-five days in the Tacoma General Hospital, fighting the pneumonia that resulted from his terrifying experience. Both of his legs were seriously injured and had to be operated upon. But six months later, walking with the aid of canes, Mr. Scott was able to return to work.

And Patches, dog-hero *extraordinaire,* was clearly the overwhelming choice to receive the coveted Gold Medal that year, for no other dog had endured so much or responded more valiantly to his master's unspoken call for help.

HERO

1966

Two-and-a-half-year-old Shawn Jolley, his short legs moving like little paddles over the floor, hurried through the kitchen to join his mother standing patiently by the door. "I got my jacket on, Mommy," Shawn said proudly, buttoning the top button of his faded blue denim jacket snugly under his chin.

Mrs. Jolley smiled at her son. She stooped down and tugged the jacket straight. Shawn was growing so fast, he would need a new one soon, she thought. "There, that's better," she said, pulling her own, matching jacket over her shoulders. "If we're going to work like ranchers, we'd better look like ranchers, don't you think?" she asked as she held open the door for Shawn, who scooted past her into the wide-open spaces of the Jolley family ranch. Shawn was too far into the yard for her to hear his reply. She followed him toward the horse barn. Midway across the yard she stopped. "Wait for me, Shawn," she called to the tow-headed boy, who had covered twice the distance she had in half the time, even though he used four times as many steps to do it. "Don't you dare go into the barn without me," she warned.

The echo of Mrs. Jolley's voice faded slowly. In the high, clear air of Idaho, miles and miles from the nearest busy town, a simple sound could be carried on the wind almost as far as the eye could see.

"Wrarf!"

Mrs. Jolley smiled. Bounding around the corner of the house, with his sleek, blue-gray fur flying like thick smoke from his streamlined frame, was Hero, next to her family Mrs. Jolley's greatest pride and joy. "Come, Hero," Mrs. Jolley called, though it was scarcely necessary, for the big collie was at her feet before she finished speaking.

The dog panted slightly as he pressed against his mistress's knees. Mrs. Jolley buried her fingers in the thick coat and scratched heartily. "Good dog," she said. "Good dog." She pulled a rough burr from Hero's mane, looked at it closely for a moment, then tossed it casually to the ground.

"Oh, Hero," she said with a trace of sadness in her voice, "what am I going to do with you? You're such a beautiful creature. You could be the Best in Show in the whole state, I just know it."

"What's keeping you, Mommy?"

Shawn was patiently waiting by the big red swinging door that was the main entrance to the horse barn. Closed, the door towered over the boy, though he could reach the handle if he stood on tiptoes.

"Coming sweetheart," Mrs. Jolley replied. She gave Hero another brisk scratch that ended in a firm, loving pat on his slender snout. "We've got work to do, boy," she said to the dog, who was moving around her legs like a ground-hugging cloud of fur. She pointed off into the distance to a dense clump of dark green trees out past the red barn and the peeling, white-painted fences that circled the property. Shadows moved beneath the trees. Horses. "Go get 'em," the ranch woman said with a sharp command.

Hero was away and flying. His feet barely touched the ground. His eyes didn't blink. He kept his long, sensitive nose aimed at the far-off grove of trees, already picking up the scent of the horses long before he could actually see them. He was a collie, born and bred to do what collies do, and he was doing it. The instinct to herd, whether it be sheep or cattle or horses was the legacy of generations of his forebears, Scottish shepherd dogs, the favorites of queens. Fleet and untiring, as graceful as an ocean wave, he bounded across the rough pasture. Hero was in his domain. The open spaces of pasture and meadow were where he was meant to be, not the prim, trim confines of the dog-show circuit—even if he were more handsome than most.

"Hero will get the horses, Shawn," Mrs. Jolley said as she pushed the heavy barn door open with a nudge of her shoulder. "You stay here with me."

Mother and son entered the barn. It was a big, open place, lined with stalls and large enough at one end to park the ranch tractor. Shawn cast a secret eye down the shadowy length of the barn to the tractor, a fascinating giant of a machine, with tires as big as upended tables and a seat so high off the floor it felt like flying when his father took him for rides.

Mrs. Jolley took Shawn by the hand. "No playing on the tractor," she said firmly. "Not today." She led Shawn to the narrow, rough-board stairs that led up to the hayloft, a cavernous, empty space bigger than two downstairs put together. Shawn went up first. His mother followed.

Shawn loved the barn. Upstairs or down, the place was a palace of boyhood delights, with more nooks and crannies and cob-webby corners than a dozen creaky house attics or a score of spooky cellars. It was his favorite place to be. While his mother pitched sweet-smelling, dust-dry hay through the hole in the hayloft floor to the horses' stalls below, Shawn ran and slid on the slippery stuff, frolicking alone as ranch children learn to do, happy to be where he was, doing what he was.

Far off across the pasture, Hero dropped down onto his belly. Creeping on his stomach, the dog inched closer and closer to the grazing horses. He didn't need the shrilly whistled commands of a shepherd or the silent arm signals of a master to give him instructions. His job was to get the horses to the barn. He knew what to do and he was doing it. He scooted closer, keeping as low as the grass around

44

him, waiting until he was as close as he could get before leaping into the air with a sharp bark.

"Wrarf!"

The chase was on. Hero was out of the grass like a shot. He raced across the remaining open space between him and the grove and circled swiftly behind the horses. They had no place to go now, except to head toward home.

The lead horse, a magnificent, huge black stallion, reared up on his hind legs in a display of regal domination and then led the herd at a trot toward the barn, quickly outdistancing the others. Hero dashed back and forth behind the stragglers, keeping the thundering pack of beautiful creatures massed together and moving along, as if they were a flock of the black-footed Colley sheep of Scotland that gave Hero's breed its name.

Mrs. Jolley paused to wipe a trickle of sweat from her forehead. She had pitched a large mound of hay through the hole in the floor and still had to distribute it to the individual horses' stalls. "That's enough for now," she said as she picked up her pitchfork and walked to the narrow stairway leading down. "Shawn," she called, waiting at the top of the stairs for her son to appear from out of the mountain of hay. "Time to go downstairs."

The loft was empty. Shawn was nowhere in sight.

At the same instant, the sound of pounding hoofs thundered like drumbeats across the wooden floor in the barn downstairs. A cold gust of wind blew up the stairs and rushed past Mrs. Jolley. The back of her neck felt as if an icy hand had touched it. *"The stallion!"* she shouted. *"He's loose in the barn!"*

Mrs. Jolley threw down the pitchfork and ran to the gaping hole in the floor, where she could look down into the barn. She opened her mouth to call for Shawn, but another sound, more chilling than the wail of a coyote beneath a winter moon, pierced the air.

"Mommy, Mommy!"

It was Shawn.

The terrified woman raced for the stairway. "Run, Shawn, run!" she screamed, knowing she was helpless to do anything for her little boy until she got down the stairs, if she could do anything for him even then. Her feet bounded down the stairs, two, three steps at a time. "Hero!" she screamed, though she had no idea where the dog was or if he was even within the sound of her frantic shout for help.

The horse maddened. He stood at one end of the empty barn pawing the air with his front hooves. On his face was a wild, red-eyed look of anger mixed with fear. Green-tinged foam hung from his lips, and flecks of it flew to his shoulders when he shook his head. And then he charged.

"Mommy!" Shawn screamed in terror at the sight of the giant animal galloping toward him. His feet were frozen to the floor in fear.

Then his eyes focused on the tractor that sat silently in the shadows across the wide floor. He knew he was small enough to slide under it and be as safe as a mouse in its hole—if only he could reach it before the huge horse trampled him down.

Shawn's legs came alive. His feet flew across the wooden floor. Running as fast as he had ever run in his young life, he made a desperate lunge for the safety of the tractor. The crazed horse was only a step behind him, its hot breath coming in loud, frightening snorts.

The tractor was within reach. Shawn ducked his head and scooted for the protected space beneath the machine, between the tractor's enormous rear wheels. Then he stopped short, as if he'd been grabbed by a giant, invisible hand.

"Oh my God!" Mrs. Jolley screamed. The edge of Shawn's denim jacket had snagged on a metal bolt projecting out from the side of the tractor. He was caught as neatly as if he'd stepped into a trap. Now there was nothing between him and the gargantuan horse that was rearing up on its hind legs, flailing the air angrily with its front hooves.

Suddenly a blur of gray-blue color streaked through the open barn door at the far end of the building and bounded off the floor in a leap that lifted it higher than the horse's head. Hero, cutting through the air in a graceful arc, his jaws opened wide to reveal cruel teeth inside, snarled a defiant challenge at the stallion and then snapped his powerful jaws closed on the tender, velvet-smooth snout of the rampaging horse.

The sudden attack by the fearless dog shifted

the horse's attention away from Shawn. Searing pain blurred the stallion's vision. Hero clung to the horse's nostrils as tightly as a lamprey to a salmon, refusing to let go. The horse shook its head violently, swinging Hero back and forth like a limp rag. But the daring dog held on. Blood began to fly from the horse's nostrils. Enraged and in pain, the horse lifted Hero high into the air, twisted him sharply to one side, and then with a sudden spin in the opposite direction, viciously hurled the dog against the side of the tractor. Hero crashed to the floor and crumpled in a furry heap.

The dog was dazed. He struggled awkwardly to his feet. He was injured and in pain, but the sight of Shawn, still pinned in terror to the tractor and within range of the horse's flying hooves, stirred the courageous dog back into action. Hero was solidly on his feet and back at the horse in an instant. He snarled and barked at the beast, snapped at its legs as they sliced by, and leaped straight into its face when it lowered its head to the floor.

Again and again the iron-rimmed hooves connected with the dog's head and body. Hero's mouth was torn and bloody. His legs were cut and bleeding. The stouthearted dog was covered with his own blood, but he continued to fight against the raging stallion without letup.

Still the horse did not slow its awesome attack. Shawn huddled in terror beneath the sweaty creature and tugged helplessly at his snagged jacket. Hero stood between the little boy and the enraged horse, refusing to budge an inch, holding steadfast to his place as guardian of the defenseless child.

Mrs. Jolley grabbed a long stick and rushed as close to the screaming, kicking horse as she dared. As Hero snapped and bit, fighting the giant with tooth and nail, his mistress poked and jabbed at it, desperately hoping to drive it off.

The horse finally dropped all four hooves to the floor and lowered its head. Its eyes became level with Hero's, who continued to watch its every move. The horse whinnied. It tossed its head as if to attack one more time, and then, with no more warning than it had given when it arrived in the barn terrifying minutes before, the giant beast whirled around and galloped majestically out of the barn door, its tail whipping in the wind.

Hero raced out the door and bounded through the yard in chase, pursuing the fleeing stallion until it was far out of sight. Then, after barking a final triumphant cry of victory that echoed all the way to the distant hills, the gallant dog slumped to the ground and a torrent of blood gushed from his mouth.

Mrs. Jolley raced to her fallen dog's side. Hero was still alive. Scooping him up in her arms, she ran with him to her car, and she and Shawn rushed their heroic pet to the veterinarian, forty-five miles away. The severely injured collie barely clung to life during the ride.

But Hero's great heart could not be stilled. In spite of serious internal damage, five broken ribs, and four knocked-out teeth, Hero survived. His injuries healed. His scars vanished beneath new growths of bushy, lustrous fur. And in five miraculous weeks, Hero, already a real champion to Shawn Jolley and his parents, was earning points in the show ring toward the coveted blue ribbon that designated the Best in Show.

But even that could not outshine the brilliant Gold Medal the stalwart collie won later that year for his daring, lifesaving battle against an enraged stallion many times his size, an incredible act of courage that certified Hero as a real-life Dog Hero of the Year.

MIJO
1967

"Come, Mijo," Feliciann Bennett called quietly. "Come, girl."

Feliciann's soft command echoed through the Bennett house, barely audible to anyone who had not been listening for it. But the young teen-ager didn't have to call again. Before the echoes died away, the soft tread of heavy paws on hardwood floors boomed a reply. Mijo, a 180-pound, short-haired St. Bernard with a solid-white chest and forelegs, a dark "tooth-brush moustache" beneath her nose, and patches over both eyes, bounded from the kitchen through the hall to where Feliciann and her younger brother Mitchell waited. Feliciann held Mijo's leash in her hand.

"Good girl," Feliciann said with a smile. She scratched Mijo behind the ears. The huge dog returned her smile with a happy, open-mouthed, tongue-wagging drool typical of her breed. "Dad said we can take you for a walk." She hooked the leather leash to Mijo's sturdy chain collar and tugged. "Come on," she said, turning toward the door. "Let's go."

The Bennett children and their huge dog were no strangers to the land surrounding their Alaskan home. The blue sky of a bright September day towered above their heads as the three romped and played and tugged and pulled at one another, racing and chasing in an endless game of "Who's Leading Whom," their antics drawing them toward the edge of a nearby water-filled gravel pit that held a special fascination for each of them.

They stopped near the rim of the pit and looked down into the giant bowl. Natural seepage plus a recent heavy rain had raised the level of water higher than it had been for weeks. Mijo tugged at the end of her leash.

"Oh, OK," Feliciann said, bending over the big dog's keglike head to undo the leash. "But the collar stays on," she added, briskly rubbing her pet under the chin where several folds of soft skin hung limp.

Free of the leash, Mijo bounded away from the two children, then spun around and returned for another hearty scratch before bounding off yet one more time.

Feliciann coiled Mijo's leash in her hand and was about to put it in her pocket when suddenly, as if the earth were being torn out from under her, the ground beneath her feet gave way and she plunged straight down into the cold water of the barren pit.

"Help!" the terrified girl screamed.

Mitchell whirled at the sound of his sister's panicked cry for help, unsure of what had happened. His eyes bugged wide when he saw she wasn't at the edge of the pit where he expected her to be.

"Help me!" Feliciann cried again.

Mitchell looked down into the pit. Feliciann was up to her neck in cold, cold water.

"I can't move," Feliciann shouted, forcing herself to shed the panic that clung to her and be calm, no matter how serious the danger. "My feet are stuck in the mud," she said almost in a whisper now, as if to shout or panic would draw her deeper into the mire and drown her. And, as if to prove the danger, when she tried to lift first one foot and then the other, freshly loosened mud swirled around them, tightening the grip around her ankles. A good swimmer, she could easily reach the safety of the firm edge of the pit if only the awful muck would let go. Panic again took hold of the young girl. It was evident that she would sink beneath the water soon if she weren't saved.

"Don't move!" Mitchell screamed at his sister. "Don't move." The young boy dashed to the edge of the pit, mindless of the fact that the rain-soaked earth could give way beneath him too and drop him to a fate similar to his sister's. He began to clamber down the steep sides of the pit.

A loud splash broke the quiet. Mijo, hearing her mistress's frantic cries of distress, had leaped off the pit's treacherous edge and plunged into the icy water, her powerful forelegs already churning in front of her.

"Oh, Mijo!" Feliciann screamed. "Come, girl! Come quick!" Mitchell stopped midway down the bank. To get any closer would put him in the same danger as Feliciann. And now it was clear that Mijo was going to try to rescue her mistress.

"Come, Mijo," Feliciann called, encouraged by the welcome sight of the big dog's head coming steadily toward her through the water. Then, without warning, the dog altered its course. She no longer headed for the stricken girl. Instead she began to swim in an aimless circle around Feliciann, whose hopes for rescue now seemed dashed.

Before the frightened girl could shout, the dog vanished under the water. The big, square, sad-faced head simply dropped out of sight.

Mitchell resumed his scramble down the bank, for he saw that once again it was up to him to save his sister. He stopped short when a shout of surprise from the pit filled the air.

"Mijo!" Feliciann cried out. "You didn't forget me."

The huge dog had dived deep under the water and then, unseen, had swum to Feliciann, coming up directly beneath her. Feliciann's fingers twined themselves tightly around Mijo's steel chain collar. Grateful that she hadn't been abandoned after all, the desperate girl clung tightly to the collar as Mijo clawed at the water with powerful strokes.

The dog pulled with the full force of its huge body, throwing every last bit of strength it could into its churning paws. Feliciann's hands, the only link between her dog's valiant efforts to free her and the powerful grip of the mud on her feet, began to slip. She closed her eyes, gritted her teeth, and managed to hold on. Mijo tugged and pulled and finally broke the mucky suction that had held Feliciann in its grip.

Once her mistress was free of the treacherous mud, Mijo wheeled around and, moving in a powerful dog paddle toward the shore, towed Feliciann to safety. Feliciann dared not let go until her huge, furry rescuer had pulled her well up onto the firm edge of the pit.

"She saved you! She saved you!" Mitchell yelled when the danger was clearly over and he too was well back from the hidden trap of eroded, crumbly soil at the pit's rim. Then the two grateful children threw their arms around Mijo and hugged the huge dog, whose heroic deed on that day would earn her the Gold Medal as the bravest dog of the year.

RINGO

1968

Mrs. Raymond Saleh was busy with her pre-Christmas holiday housecleaning when a plaintive whine, barely heard over the ordinary hums and buzzes of a busy house, caught her attention. She tipped her head to listen. The sound, whatever it was and whatever was making it, came from the back door. Mrs. Saleh crossed the kitchen and stopped just inside the closed door. There was definitely something outside. She pushed open the door cautiously, her right hand holding tightly to the broom she carried. Very carefully she stuck her head out the door and slowly turned this way and that, searching her yard from one end to the other to discover the source of the noise. The yard was empty. With a puzzled look, Mrs. Saleh stepped back inside and began to close the door.

"Rrruuu?"

"Oh! My goodness!" the startled woman exclaimed, staring down in surprise at a bundle on the back doorstep. "Where on earth did you come from?"

Sitting on the step, no larger than a skein of fuzzy brown-and-white yarn, was a pitiful little puppy with big brown eyes and a coal-black nose scratching weakly against the door. "Rru," the puppy whined in a call so feeble it might have been a squeaky hinge on a troublesome door.

Mrs. Saleh shook her head. She folded her arms across her chest. The puppy continued to scratch and whine on the other side of the door. Mrs. Saleh's four children weren't home, but they were due soon. If they came home and found the dog on their step, she would never be rid of it. "And just when we ordered a dog for the children's Christmas surprise," she sighed, undecided about what to do. "Well, we simply can't have two dogs around here," she said, grasping the door handle firmly in one hand and her broom tightly in the other. She hesitated for a moment, unable to put her heart into what she had to do next. But two dogs were out of the question. She took a deep breath and pushed open the door wide.

"Shoo!" she shouted at the puppy. "Go 'way. Go home."

The puppy's eyes grew large. It stopped pawing the door. It began to cower, lowering itself so close to the ground that not even a speck of dust could have gotten under its shivering belly. "You heard me," Mrs. Saleh said, not too convincingly. "Now, shoo!" She waved her broom again at the puppy.

The puppy tumbled off the step and rolled onto its side. It lay still for just a moment and then rose clumsily to its feet and scooted around the corner of the house in terror, its fuzzy tail curled tightly between its legs.

Though uncomfortable about having chased the puppy away, Mrs. Saleh was still determined to finish her work before her family arrived home. She hurried to the garage where she kept her cleaning supplies. As she entered the empty garage, a flurry of movement in the back corner caught her attention. The puppy was back. It was tugging weakly at the ragged, floppy end of a mop that leaned against the wall. The tiny creature was so hungry it was trying to eat the mop.

"Oh, you poor little dear," Mrs. Saleh exclaimed. She scooped up the puppy in her hands, pressed it tightly to her, and carried it quickly into the house. "I don't care if we ordered a basset hound for the children or not. No helpless little thing like you is going to go hungry if I have anything to say about it," she said soothingly.

Mrs. Saleh filled a big dish with food and placed it on the kitchen floor. Next to it she set a saucer of milk, and next to that a dish of fresh water. As soon as she put the puppy on the floor, it buried its nose in the food and didn't stop eating or drinking until every dish was empty. Mrs. Saleh smiled, her guilt about having chased the little dog away now completely vanished.

When the children came home they found the puppy all curled up, sound asleep, in a satisfied heap on the rug. "That's our dog," they shouted happily. "It's exactly the dog we wanted."

Mr. and Mrs. Saleh stood side by side, watching their children pet and play with the uninvited guest. "I guess we got our Christmas pup after all," Mr. Saleh said.

Mrs. Saleh nodded approvingly. "Maybe he's a little early and a little on the ragged side," she said, "but there he is."

When it came time to name the new family member, the children studied their dog carefully. Nobody could tell just exactly what kind of a dog he was. Even the veterinarian who gave the pup his shots wasn't certain, though he speculated that the furry, fast-growing brown-and-white mutt was at least part St. Bernard, with perhaps a little chow thrown in. But nobody really cared. Certainly not the Salehs. So, with nothing more to go by than what he looked like, the Saleh children decided to name their new pup Ringo, because he had a pure-white mane of thick, glossy fur in a ring around his neck and because the Beatles were popular at the time.

Ringo grew by leaps and bounds. From the tiny, six-week-old pup who had trouble out-wrestling a kitchen mop, Ringo grew into a big, handsome creature who, if he had the mind to, could hold a full-grown man at bay. And even more, as time would soon tell.

It was after Ringo had reached his full growth that little Randy Saleh, just two-and-a-half years old, one day wandered away from home. Randy was a fun-loving boy who enjoyed most of all to roam the yards and empty lots of his Euless, Texas, neighborhood. The wide-open spaces of the small town situated between Dallas and Ft. Worth weren't quite wide open enough to suit the adventurous Randy. In fact, only minutes before he wandered off, his father was preparing to install a gate that would keep the lad safely in bounds. But it was too late. Randy was gone. He vanished as completely as if he'd fallen down a prairie-dog hole.

The police were called in at once. A search was organized. For two solid hours the neighborhood was combed thoroughly from one end to the other. But there wasn't a trace of the wanderer—or his dog.

Nearly a mile away, Harley Jones, a maintenance man at a local school, was on his way home from work. He was suddenly forced to step down hard on the brakes of his car. Traffic on Pipeline Road, often very busy and quite dangerous but usually steady moving, had come to a halt in his lane as it approached a blind curve in the road. A long line of cars stretched all the way to the curve, more than forty cars in all. The drivers sat impatiently behind their wheels. Traffic was at a standstill. Harley got out of his car to see what the holdup was. He walked to the next car in line. "What's up?" he asked the driver ahead of him. "Accident?" "Nope," the man replied. "Somebody said something about a mad dog in the street."

"Mad dog?" Harley asked, scratching his head. "This I've got to see." He proceeded to walk to the head of the line. All along the way the other drivers warned him to be careful. "Mad dog in the road up ahead," they said from the safety of their cars. "Better stay in your car."

Harley Jones hesitated as he neared the curve. He could hear the enraged, snarling howls of a dog, no question about it. But he had to see for himself. He rounded the curve.

"Great day in the morning!" he exclaimed, stunned by the sight that greeted him. There in the center of the busy road, his white mane flowing gracefully as he leaped back and forth from one side to the other, was a mongrel dog. It was Ringo! The dog had blocked traffic completely. The moment a car made a tentative move to go, Ringo would leap at it, snarling and barking and throwing himself against its fender. He repeated this strange behavior over and over again. No driver would dare enter the territory now claimed by a very determined and seemingly very angry dog. For some reason that Harley Jones and none of the other stalled drivers could fathom, the mongrel dog was forbidding traffic to continue past the curve in the road.

Jones inched his way forward along the sides of the cars, using them as a shield. When he reached the front car, nothing stood between him and the dog. But he was still unable to see around the blind corner. Ringo glared at him. Then, for some reason Jones didn't understand, the dog raced around the curve, out of sight. But he was gone for only a moment before he returned, just as mean-looking as ever. And the moment the bushy dog reappeared, he threw himself at the front car, which had taken the opportunity of his brief absence to creep ahead a few feet. The car stopped. And again Ringo dashed around the curve out of sight.

Jones puzzled over the dog's confusing, inexplicable behavior. "Something strange is going on around that corner," he mused aloud, "and I aim to see what it is." He inched cautiously forward. Ringo scowled at him. The man moved step by careful step closer to the curve. The dog pounced on a moving car. Its driver jammed on the brakes. Ringo vanished around the corner. He returned. It was all a very curious thing to Harley Jones, who quietly moved ahead each time the dog's attention was given to directing traffic.

Jones hesitated for a moment when he reached the curve. Another few steps and he would be able to see what the excited dog was hiding. He peered furtively around the corner while Ringo was momentarily out of sight.

"My stars!" Jones exclaimed. He put his hand

to his forehead and rubbed his eyes in wonder. There, plunked down in the middle of the road with a big, happy grin on his face, was a little boy— Randy—playing on the street as if he were safe in his own backyard.

Suddenly Ringo came bounding around the corner, barking at the top of his lungs. Randy giggled at the dog, who hurried to his side and stood squarely on all fours, facing Jones, who didn't dare move a step closer. The dog's fangs were bared and he was snarling. Clearly he was protecting the little boy.

As Jones watched in wide-eyed amazement, Ringo buried his muzzle in the child's side and began to push. The heavy dog outweighed and outpowered the boy, who reluctantly scooted to the side of the road on his hands and knees. The moment Randy was out of danger, Ringo raced back around the corner to the line of stalled traffic. Jones kept a wary eye on the dog but inched cautiously toward the child.

Randy thought he and Ringo were playing a wonderful game. While the mongrel was gone, the boy dashed right back into the middle of the roadway and sat down. He laughed aloud when Ringo reappeared, panting and puffing in exhaustion from the nonstop exertion of rushing back and forth. Once more the dog nudged the little boy to safety at the side of the road.

Jones stared, unable to believe the amazing

dedication the big dog showed to the fun-loving child. And each time the dog was busy holding back traffic, Jones moved a few steps closer to the child, who continued to scurry into the road to play the moment the dog left him alone.

For fifteen harrowing minutes the dog, the boy, the man, and the line of traffic continued to repeat this hair-raising sequence of events. Jones was afraid to move quickly. The dog's snapping jaws and angry growls made it clear what would happen if he lunged.

"Nice dog," Jones said over and over in a soothing voice. "That's a nice dog." He spoke in quiet, reassuring tones to the frantic animal. At last, after long, anxious minutes, Jones was able to reach Randy, who was once more plunked down directly in the line of any car that might come screeching around the corner without warning. He grabbed Randy up in his arms and gingerly stepped to the side of the road. Ringo growled menacingly at Jones's legs each step of the way until, at last, all three were safely off the road. Then Ringo relaxed. The first car appeared from around the blind corner. The dog didn't give it a second look. His job was done. The car whizzed by, followed by another and then another. Soon the entire parade of cars was back to normal on busy Pipeline Road.

Very few of the puzzled, impatient drivers ever knew what had been delaying them. None knew that

Ringo, a very special Christmas dog who had appeared out of nowhere, had saved the life of his young master. It was an act of heroism that would gain him the Gold Medal and the much-deserved recognition as Dog Hero of the Year.

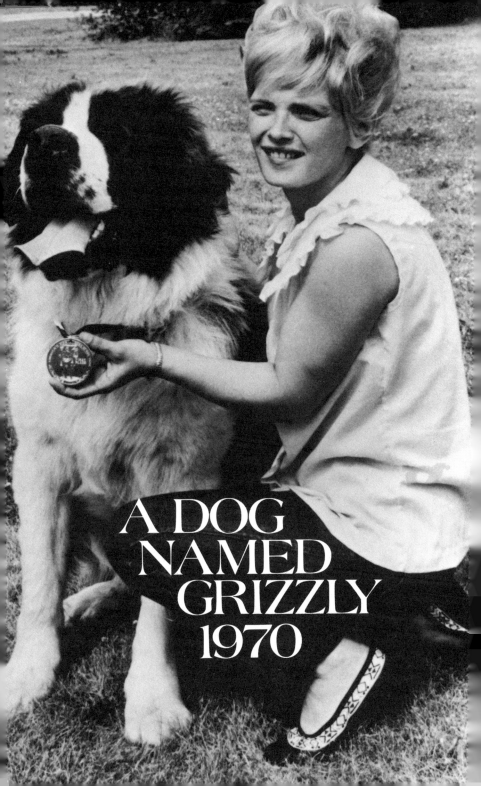

A DOG
NAMED
GRIZZLY
1970

The sharp crack of a dry tree branch snapping echoed through the crisp spring air. Before the sound of the first crack died away, it was followed by another, and then another. Littered with fallen trees and dead branches, the forest floor was no longer cushioned by a thick layer of snow. Most of the deep snow of winter had melted. Anyone or anything walking through the woods could not avoid crushing the branches that lay scattered about like the gray skeletons of long-dead beasts. The crunching, cracking noises continued. Then they stopped.

"Arrunnk."

A grizzly bear, shaggy-coated and thin from a long, hard winter, stopped in the shadow of a huge pine tree that marked the edge of the forest. Below, down a gentle slope, was a vast clearing. In the center of the clearing, basking in the warm glow of the noonday Alaskan sun, stood a lodge made of rough-hewn timber and still sporting a rooftop covered with sparkling white snow. The grizzly bear sniffed the air. Traces of smoke, which rose in a thin blue line from a central stone chimney of the lodge, drifted up the slope. The bear sniffed again as the faint cloud vanished and the air around grew clear again. The bear's eyes flickered back and forth across the clearing. There was another smell in the air that gripped her attention. It too was coming from the lodge. Somewhere in that forbidden place inhabited by humans there was food.

The grizzly bear rolled her mammoth head over her shoulder and growled. Then she grunted again.

From the dark shadows of the deep woods came the answer of another bear's grunt. But the second was not nearly so loud as the first bear's. In fact, it was so faint that only someone listening closely for it would have heard. The first bear growled again. This time there was no reply. Instead, the sound of cracking and crunching issued from the woods, followed in an instant by a grizzly bear cub making its first journey to join its mother at the threatening edge of a human domain.

The young cub stopped at its mother's side. The older bear towered over the cub, who peered inquisitively down the hill toward the lodge. The mother bear was more than five feet tall at the shoulder as she stood on all fours, much taller than a young child standing up straight would be. The cub ambled to the edge of the clearing. It sniffed the air and smelled the delicious aroma of food. Food was what the two bears were looking for. The cub darted ahead. In seconds it was half-tumbling, half-romping down the hill, tripping over its own huge paws with its snout pointing steadily toward the lodge.

In the kitchen of a cabin behind the lodge, Mrs. David Gratias, who with her husband owned the main lodge, was preparing the noon meal for Mr. Gratias and their little daughter, Theresa. Mr. Gratias was tending to the many chores that were constantly in need of doing around the place. He would come for lunch when he was called—provided, of course, that he wasn't too far off to hear.

Theresa, just two years old, was sound asleep in the front room near the door of the comfortable family cabin.

As she worked alone in the kitchen, Mrs. Gratias thought she heard a noise coming from somewhere in the clearing behind the cabin. She paused for a moment and stopped her chopping of the big white onion she had just selected from the root cellar. Spring in Alaska meant the arrival of fresh food. Mrs. Gratias was glad the long winter would soon be over.

"Oh, it's probably just the wind," she said, but cast a quick glance across the kitchen to where the family dog lay sleeping in a lazy, furry heap. The dog didn't stir, and so Mrs. Gratias forgot about the noise and went on with her meal preparation.

But the dog wasn't exactly sleeping. He had heard the noise too and was listening. His sharp senses quickened. Though he was still something of a puppy, only twenty months old, years of fine breeding caused him to be alert. St. Bernards are not only excellent rescue dogs, they are fine watchdogs as well. Though not yet full-grown, the Gratias's dog was so large that he had already outstripped his official name and had acquired a new name more fitting of his size and weight. He was called, simply, Grizzly Bear.

Grizzly Bear didn't look or act like a real bear. His big, sad-happy face and docile temperament were nothing at all like the menacing look and unfriendly disposition of a real grizzly, one of the largest and fiercest of all wild creatures. Instead, he was a friendly, easygoing, and gentle family pet. Like most of his breed, Grizzly Bear was rather clumsy-looking and, given his choice, somewhat lazy indoors. But he had come from a long line of heroic ancestors, huge mountain dogs that had been bred to rescue lost travelers in the Swiss Alps. Alaska was a fitting place for a St. Bernard called Grizzly Bear.

Grizzly rolled a sleepy eye toward the kitchen door and listened. He was familiar with the sounds of the kitchen, the comings and goings at the lodge, and the strange, peculiar silence of the surrounding forest. The sound he heard was not familiar. He sniffed the air. The pungent aroma of onion caught him by surprise. He winced.

Mrs. Gratias again paused and this time put her knife down on the cutting board. She turned her ear toward the window. "I *do* hear a noise," she exclaimed aloud. "There's something in the yard."

Grizzly's ears were perked. He no longer lay in slumber. He sat up in a crouch, watching his mistress.

"It's probably nothing more than some birds fighting over scraps," Mrs. Gratias said, again out loud. "But I better take a look, just to be sure." She started walking toward the front door, the only entrance to the cabin, when she noticed that Grizzly was sitting up. The dog, leashed to a heavy table, was looking at her eagerly. "Oh, all right," Mrs. Gratias said, and she turned back and untied the leash. "You might as well get some exercise too. At the rate you're growing, you're going to be too big to get back inside the cabin before long." She laughed and went to the door.

As Mrs. Gratias stepped outside into the sunlight, she glanced back at Theresa, who continued to sleep soundly near the door. She smiled warmly at her tiny daughter. Instead of closing the door, she left it open just a crack.

The air was brisk and refreshing. Mrs. Gratias hugged herself to keep warm as she walked to the rear of the cabin. As she neared the backyard, she paused to listen. Clearly, something was in the yard behind the house. She stepped boldly around the corner to see what it could be.

"Oh, my goodness!" Mrs. Gratias's arms came up in surprise. She stopped dead in her tracks. Rum-

maging near the back wall of the cabin, scraggly and very hungry-looking, was the grizzly bear cub. The cub was just as startled as she.

"Arrunnk," the cub grunted.

The sound was enough to shock Mrs. Gratias to the awful truth of what she had stumbled upon. She knew enough about the wilds of Alaska to know that grizzly bear cubs are seldom very far from their mothers. She also knew that a mother bear separated from her cub was one of the most dangerous and fearsome creatures in the world.

"Theresa!" Mrs. Gratias screamed, suddenly remembering that she had left the front door ajar. She whirled on the snow-covered ground and raced toward the front of the house. She had to get to the door and make sure that Theresa was safe. Nothing else mattered.

The instant she rounded the corner of the house, her worst fears came alive. The mother grizzly, looking for her own wandering offspring, stood face to face with the terrified woman.

"David!" Mrs. Gratias screamed in horror. But her cry for her husband was smothered by the rumbling snarl of the angry bear.

The bear reared up onto her hind legs. She was immense. Her head stood higher than the eaves of the cabin. She towered over the woman. She was so huge that she blocked out the sun.

Panic momentarily gripped Mrs. Gratias. The bear, a solid wall of shaggy-furred, hungry beast, blocked the way between her and Theresa, who was still inside the open door. There was only one thought on Mrs. Gratias's mind. She had to protect her daughter.

Mrs. Gratias leaped sideways, desperately trying to get around the bear who stood above her with menacing paws slashing the air. But Mrs. Gratias slipped on the icy ground beneath her feet and fell solidly to the frozen earth, striking her head sharply on the rock-hard surface. Her vision blurred. She was totally helpless now.

The mammoth beast dropped to all fours and set upon her.

Driven by instinct to protect her cub which she could not see, the grizzly bear raked her massive claws across Mrs. Gratias's face. Blood poured from the wound. Another slash tore the flesh of the helpless woman's shoulder. Then the giant bear opened her huge mouth wider than a man's head, and with ivory teeth glistening with saliva, prepared to inflict the fatal bite.

Mrs. Gratias struggled, but she was already badly wounded and much too weak to fend off the crazed animal. The giant head came toward her. The razor-sharp teeth were only inches away.

Then, without warning, there was a flash of brown-and-white fur in the air. The huge bear grunted aloud as Grizzly, all 180 pounds of him, crashed headlong into her chest. The sudden blow knocked the enraged beast away from Grizzly's fallen mistress. The bear staggered backwards, stunned by the powerful flying leap of the attacking dog.

The bear's attention was no longer on the fallen woman, who weakly struggled to regain her feet. Instead, the wild creature's wrath was directed toward the dog. The bear roared. Her huge lips curled. Fangs sharp as knives sparkled white against the red flesh of her mouth. Mingled in the red was Mrs. Gratias's own blood. She had been severely injured.

The beast bellowed. Yet the faithful, bold, and daring Grizzly, his own fangs no match for the giant's, jumped and darted back and forth between the towering beast and her intended victim. The bear couldn't get close to the downed woman. Each time she tried to move forward, Grizzly barked and leaped at the creature, driving her back. Grizzly snapped at the bear's massive paws and repeatedly struck her in the head and chest with solid blows from his thick paws. He refused to let the bear advance a step closer to the moaning woman lying dazed on the ground.

Mrs. Gratias watched in horror the terrible battle between the real grizzly bear and her own beloved Grizzly. Fur flew and blood spattered across the sparkling snow. Mrs. Gratias grew weaker. Her vision again blurred. Loss of blood and sheer terror over the awful ordeal still raging around her overwhelmed her. She lapsed into unconsciousness as the howling battle between the beasts went on.

A few moments later, Mrs. Gratias blinked her

eyes open. There was silence. The bright yellow sun was shining down on her. She could feel its pleasant warmth on her back. She felt the cold snow beneath her and knew she was alive. As she painfully raised her head, she thought she saw another flash of fur, and the image of the crazed bear returning to finish her off caused her heart to leap. But something warm and wet caressed her cheek. Mrs. Gratias blinked her eyes open again. Grizzly, his fur torn and spattered with blood, put his big, sad face next to that of his mistress and licked her wounds.

"Grizzly," Mrs. Gratias murmured. The awful events just concluded were still unclear in her mind. Then she remembered!

"Theresa!" she screamed as she struggled to her feet. The terror was still not over. What if the bear wasn't really gone? She staggered to the front of the cabin. The door was open.

Grizzly bounded past Mrs. Gratias and leaped through the open door, his big furry tail wagging rapidly to and fro. This sight was all the reassurance the panicked mother needed.

"She's all right," Mrs. Gratias gasped in relief, holding onto the open door for support. "Theresa is all right." She peered into the friendly warmth of her cozy cabin home. Theresa lay sound asleep, exactly where her mother had left her. And curled up alongside the little girl, bloody, torn, and frightfully dirty but with his tail wagging happily as if nothing had happened, was Grizzly.

Mrs. Gratias threw her arms around the big,

bold dog. Tears of overwhelming gratitude filled her eyes. "You saved both our lives, Grizzly," she said, hugging him tightly, "Theresa's and mine."

And later that year, the amazing dog named Grizzly Bear was awarded the Dog Hero of the Year Gold Medal.

TRIXIE
1971

"Where is Ricky?"

Mrs. Richard Sherry bolted out the back door of her house and ran into the yard. She zipped the front of her jacket all the way up, to keep out the chill of the spring wind. Something was terribly wrong. She could sense it. Her eyes darted anxiously from one corner of the yard to the other, following the unbroken line of sturdy fence surrounding it. A child's sled, its runners showing rust, lay forgotten in a corner of the yard, a reminder of the winter that was just past.

"No!" the worried mother gasped. Her eyes were no longer moving. They were fixed on a small hole in the fence, just large enough for a dog, or a small child, to pass through.

"Ricky!" Mrs. Sherry screamed. There was no answer to her call.

Ricky Sherry ambled gaily down Buchanan Bridge Road, his small booted feet making designs in the sand left by the sanding trucks of winter. It was too cold a day to go to the beach to play, but kicking the dusty sand that lay in small heaps along the edge of the road was almost as good. Ricky giggled and laughed. The wind blew across his face, stirring the brown curls poking out from beneath his cap. He was bundled warmly at his mother's insistence in a sturdy, aqua-colored jacket and didn't mind the brisk weather at all. After all, it was spring. For a two-year-old, it was a day of perfect adventure after a long, cold Massachusetts winter.

Trotting at his side was Trixie, the Sherry family dog. Trixie, who was almost as big as the boy she followed, was a roly-poly black-and-white mongrel, of a mixed breed that nobody had ever bothered to guess the ancestry of. She was a short-haired dog, with floppy ears, mostly white, some dark spots on her back, and a black mask over her head and eyes that made her look as if someone had pulled a hat over her face. Trixie followed Ricky down Buchanan Bridge Road, avoiding the sudden clouds of sand kicked up by the happy little boy as he drew closer and closer to Buchanan Bridge Pond, a deep and frigid body of water that only recently had been covered with thick ice.

Ricky stopped at the pond and drew close to its edge, so he could look at his reflection on the surface of the coal-black water. Trixie appeared in the mirrorlike image, standing at his side. "Trixie," Ricky said with a laugh, pointing at the wavy reflection. He threw a pebble at the water. The images shimmered and broke up into many tiny reflections. Ricky giggled and reached for another pebble as the mirror likenesses settled back to normal. He drew his arm back to pitch the second pebble far out into the pond, but his foot struck a greasy patch of mud. *"Oh!"* he cried out, as both feet slipped out from under him and he went tumbling down the short bank into the water.

Trixie leaped to the edge of the bank. But the small boy in the pale green-blue jacket was already gone. Ripples of murky water closed over the spot where he had sunk. Ricky Sherry was already on the muddy bottom of Buchanan Bridge Pond.

"He must have crawled through the hole in the fence," Mrs. Sherry said in between short, nervous breaths. She was addressing a small group of neighbors who had assembled the moment it was known that Ricky was missing. "He can't have gone far," she said hopefully. "He was wearing his aqua jacket and. . . ." The distraught mother couldn't go on. "We've just got to find him," she said.

The group of searchers immediately spread out over the neighborhood, calling for the lost boy as they went. They poked their heads into empty garages and looked vainly into thickets of bushes. They combed yard after yard, yet listened with each step for the shout that would tell them Ricky had been found. But no such cry came.

Mrs. Manna, the Sherrys' next-door neighbor, hurried in the direction of Buchanan Bridge Pond. Her head turned from side to side, looking for the flash of green that would be Ricky's jacket. A distant sound greeted her ears. It grew close very fast. It was the sharp bark of a dog. Mrs. Manna stopped to listen.

Trixie bolted into view. She was sopping wet, a long trail of water droplets marking her desperate race from the pond's muddy bank. She yapped and barked ceaselessly and howled as if she were in agony.

"What is it, Trixie?" Mrs. Manna shouted over the barks of the dog.

The madly yapping dog whirled on the gravel and, cutting through backyards, raced headlong through the neighborhood back toward the pond. Mrs. Manna followed the frantic animal at a full run, keeping up with Trixie as best she could.

An icy knife of terror plunged through the frightened woman's rapidly beating heart when she saw Trixie stop at the edge of the cold, silent pond. *"Not the pond!"* she cried, gasping for breath.

Trixie ran up and down along the water's edge, barking without stop. Mrs. Manna hurried to the bank of the pond. She peered out over the icy water. The surface of the pond was unbroken. "There's nothing floating out there," she said.

Trixie didn't waste another second. Unable to

communicate what she knew had happened, the frustrated dog leaped into the water and paddled a short distance out into the pond. She barked and barked again without stop as she swam around and around in a tight circle.

Mrs. Manna stepped as close to the water's edge as she could, squinting to see through the murky depths for a glimpse of anything at all in the water. Her hand flew to her mouth as a tiny fleck of light-green color, hardly distinguishable from the water surrounding it, broke the surface. *"Ricky's jacket!"* she screamed. She instantly plunged into the bitter-cold pond and plowed through the misty water to where Trixie continued to circle the bit of green cloth.

Mrs. Manna lunged at the cloth. Her hands closed tightly around something solid. It was the apparently lifeless form of a small boy, drifting just beneath the shiny surface of the pond.

The horrified woman struggled for shore, clutching the little boy's limp body in her arms. Ricky's eyes were closed. He wasn't breathing. Even his heart had stopped.

Firemen responding to the emergency call were on the scene in moments. They worked feverishly to resuscitate the boy, forcing unbelievable amounts of water from his small lungs. But still no signs of life appeared to encourage them. They continued their efforts, refusing to give up, as an ambulance rushed Ricky to Lynn Hospital. There a team of skilled physicians, alerted to the emergency, waited for his arrival.

It was not known how long Ricky had been underwater. It was not known how long he had gone without breathing or at what moment his tiny heart had stopped. Ricky's body temperature was only 60°, far, far below normal. There appeared to be no conceivable way the little boy could be saved. But the doctors, like the determined firemen, refused to give up.

Using every method known to them, the doctors slowly raised Ricky's body temperature to 83°. Suddenly, to everyone's great surprise and delight, Ricky's heart began beating for the first time in at least twenty minutes. He was alive!

The doctors worked around the clock. They gradually warmed their small patient's body so that by noon on the day after the accident, it was back to normal. Ricky was saved.

But the ordeal wasn't over. Another fear gripped the hearts and minds of all those who had heard of the dreadful incident. It was well-known that whenever a person's heart stops beating for as long as Ricky's had, the inevitable result is brain damage. There was a strong possibility, then, that the near-drowning had left Ricky damaged for life.

For a solid week the medical team closely monitored their little miracle patient. Then the verdict came in. There was no brain damage! In fact, there wasn't the slightest bit of physical or mental damage at all! Ricky was as good as new.

When Ricky returned home at last from his harrowing adventure, he was greeted by a welcoming crowd of happy neighbors. But the loudest and happiest greeting of all came from a noisily barking black-and-white, flop-eared mongrel, the brave and brilliant dog who had saved Ricky's life. Trixie, as she so deserved, was the Gold Medal winner of the year.

ABOUT THE AUTHOR

D. J. Arneson, a former editor for Dell Publishing, is now a free-lance writer. He is the author of one novel for adults, *Walk to Survival* (Ace Books) and approximately thirty-five books for young readers.

D. J. is married, has two sons, and makes his home in Southbury, Connecticut.